clown

farmer

bulldozer operator

lobster fishermonsters

doctor

salesmonster

street sweeper

captain

librarian

yeoman

photographer

television camera-monster

automobile mechanic

golfer

to
Doug Cushman
who paints a mean brush

Little Monster at Work

By Mercer Mayer

MERRIGOLD PRESS • NEW YORK

Contents

One day, Little Monster said, "Grandpa, Grandpa, what will I be when I grow up?"

"Come with me," said Grandpa,
"and we'll find out."

First, Little Monster helped build a road.

motor grader

dynamiter

Boom

detonator

line painter

concrete pipe

THIS WAY TO

PETE'S PLACE

hydraulic excavator

That's my boy!

THEIRS

lunch box

ROADS ARE UNFAIR TO RABBITS

May I go to the bathroom?

plans

stadia rod

transit

surveyor

surveyor's helper

11

Next, Little Monster tried a job working with cars.

news anchormonsters

VERY BAD

The GREEDY GOURMET

MONSTER AT THE MOVIES

LATE NEWS

EARLY NEWS

phooey

camera 3

camera 4

news desk

studio electrician

klieg light

rain

snow

sun

cold

hot

100% LOW ACCURATE

38°

HI

72°

300°

-4

Then he became a TV star.

sponsor

floor speaker

THE RAIN WILL BE WET.

YESTERDAY'S WEATHER TODAY

TROLLUSK BROTH...3-RING...

Hey, Grandpa, Lookit me.

TROLLUSK BROS. CIRCUS

tightrope walkers and riders

trapeze artists

program vender

juggler

tent pole

bareback rider

trapeze

At the circus, Little Monster's clown act was a smash hit.

THE NEWS
YOU LIKE TO HEAR

darkroom

darkroom
technician

chemicals

enlarger

sportswriter

typewriter

staff artist

draw
board

business analyst

editor in chief

water
cooler

copyboy

society
columnist

ticker tape machine

linotype
machine

printing
press

delivery
monster

RING

operator

pressmonster

With the story of his clown act on the front page, Little Monster thought he might try the newspaper business.

19

It was time for Little Monster's check-up, so he and Grandpa went straight to the Monsterville Medical Center.

space shuttle

solar cells

Herbie,
Emilia
Wingba
She's f...

Explorer
satellite

asteroids

ISLAND JOE'S
MOON RESORT

TV
transmi...

launch
director

mathematician

telescope

HERMES II

lunar
rover

rocket

moon
wheelbarrow

astronomer

rocket
technician

moon
rock
collector

moon science
colony

launching
pad

. . . he went to the moon,
to be an astronaut.

THE MOON

At the airport, Little Monster
visited the control tower.

33

"Maybe I'll be a scientist and study something," said Little Monster.

MUMMY'S BOY

Kiss me and I'll turn into a prince.

He told me that, too, and look what happened to me.

archeologist (studies people of long ago)

ichthyologist (studies fishes)

monsterologist (studies you-know-what)

35

It just so happened that the great
Crafts Fair was going on that day.
"I love to make things, Grandpa,"
said Little Monster. "Let's take a look."

basket weaver

hand press

printer

brayer

rug maker

dye vat

dyer

bellows

forge

blacksmith

anvil

loom

knitter

weaver

yarn

41

42

It was time for dinner, so
Grandpa and Little Monster
headed for home.

43

The next day . . .

businessmonster

44